DreamWorks®
MONSTERS
VS
ALIENS
™

In this EXCITING issue...

EXPOSED! SECRET GOV'T PRISON FOR MONSTERS

ALIEN ROBOT ON RAMPAGE IN SAN FRAN!

PLUS

- Chilling Eyewitness Interviews
- Exclusive Photos
- Declassified Documents

HarperCollins®, ☰®, and HarperEntertainment® are trademarks of HarperCollins Publishers.

Monsters vs. Aliens: Meet the Monsters
Monsters vs. Aliens ™ & © 2009 DreamWorks Animation L.L.C.

Printed in the United States of America.

Library of Congress catalog card number is available.
ISBN 978-0-06-156724-7
Designed by Rick Farley and Joe Merkel
❖
First Edition

DREAMWORKS
MONSTERS VS ALIENS™

MEET THE MONSTERS

Adapted by N. T. Raymond

HARPER ◗ ENTERTAINMENT

An Imprint of HarperCollinsPublishers

SUNNY DAYS AHEAD FOR WEATHERMAN AND BRIDE-TO-BE

Channel 172 weatherman Derek Dietl will marry his sweetheart, Susan Murphy, next week. When asked how both the bride and groom were feeling as their big day approached, the *Good Morning, Modesto* star said, "We're feeling clear and sunny with a high of 72!"

Susan Murphy on her BIG day

HERE COM
MI

ES THE BRIDEZILLA
TEOR CRASHES WEDDING

A meteor crashed into the wedding of Modesto weatherman Derek Dietl and fiancée Susan Murphy. The uninvited guest bounced off the bride and knocked her out for a spell.

Once she came to, Murphy insisted she was fine. But according to witnesses, the bride glowed green and the mysterious space rock transformed her into a five-story-tall bride with white hair. Her big day was *really* big.

The Modesto meteor

MISSING MURPHY

Government Hides Giant Bride

EXCLUSIVE PHOTOS

A maximum-security government facility was *not* where Susan Murphy planned to spend her honeymoon. The army has taken her to an unnamed top secret compound in the desert.

"She's just changed so much since the wedding," said bridesmaid Kelly Brown. "She's not the Susan I used to know."

> **"She's just changed so much since the wedding."**

Sources report that the government has renamed the small-town sweetheart "Ginormica." And no wonder! Her extreme makeover left her standing 49 feet, 11 inches tall. And not only is she a giant, but she is super strong, too. The army needed helicopters and tanks to take her down.

General W. R. Monger was recently asked for information about the secret government compound.

"Don't you know it's illegal to even mention that place? I mean . . . uh, no such place exists. I have no further comment."

General W. R. Monger denies everything

GENERAL DENIES EXISTENCE OF MONSTER PRISON

ASTRONOMERS
NOTICE STRANGE BLIP

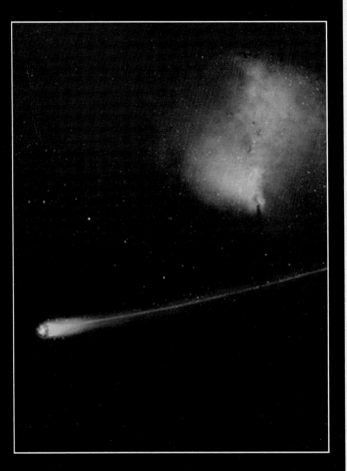

Astronomers announced yesterday the sighting of an unidentified bright light racing across the night sky. Investigations into the matter are ongoing.

Top secret government files were recently released to the public, and they contain startling reports of other monsters captured in years past.

In the files, local eyewitnesses report sightings of a tall man with the head of a cockroach. The hideous creature was very polite and quiet when going through the garbage of all the homes on Sequoia Avenue.

"He couldn't get enough of my compost pile, but got very distracted when he saw the encyclopedias I'd put out on the porch for recycling," said area resident Brett Bigglesworth.

The files reveal the creature to be Dr. Cockroach, PhD, the result of a failed science experiment intended to endow humans with the genetic longevity of cockroaches.

SECRET FILES OPENED!

Ginormica Is Not the Only Monster Around

BEFORE

AFTER

The polite pest

More Secret Files Reveal
THE MISSING LINK!

Like something out of an old horror movie, the existence of a bizarre creature in our midst has been revealed by recently declassified files. Eyewitnesses who originally reported a rather unusual disturbance years ago are just now coming forth.

"I was at the pool working on my tan, when this . . . this beast accosted me. It seemed like they were letting in all kinds of riffraff in those days," said Muffy Danforth, a member of the elite Wellington Country Club.

It turns out the riffraff Ms. Danforth was referring to was none other than the evolutionary marvel known as The Missing Link. Half-ape, half-fish, Mr. Link is the only surviving evidence of the evolutionary connection between prehistoric man and our undersea ancestors.

TOP SECRET

CONFI

Newly Released Dossier "Clears" Up Sightings

Several Almost-sightings
Leave Witnesses Confused

Buried in piles of government files were eyewitness reports and lab analyses confirming yet another monster on Earth!

Adam Mac and his brother John were grilling in their backyard when they spotted a transparent thing moving in their neighbor's yard. "He was clear like a jellyfish," said Adam. Later analysis of the substance left behind on the grass proved to be Bicarbonate Ostylezene Benzoate.

A group of high school girls confirmed the sighting. "He introduced himself as B.O.B.," Sherry Perkins said. "We thought he was kinda cute, in an oozing way." Perkins and her friends said B.O.B. enjoyed his time at their pool party until he forgot how to float and how to breathe. After they told him to "suck in, blow out," he recovered but said he should go home and lie down. No one could report where "home" was.

WHAT'S THE BUZZ?

Quackenmeyer claims this is a photo of the mystery creature

Desert-area residents have filed numerous noise complaints about loud screeching in their community for weeks, but no one has been able to detect the source. Orlando Quackenmeyer, self-proclaimed local historian and conspiracy theorist, claims this occurrence also ties in to the reports about the secret government prison facility in the desert.

"It's a giant grub," he says. "I call him Screecher but his official name is Insectosaurus. He's been captive ever since he was a little larva. He loves bright lights, strobes especially, so light 'em up if you want to see him. I even got a picture of him. He's very large so it was hard to fit all of him in the photo."

The President Calls for Calm

The President asks citizens of the nation to stay calm as news of monsters being held in a top secret compound spreads.

"I have my eye on the ball, and there is no giant monster ball out there," President Hathaway assured the public.

ALIENS ATTACK!

If Headed to San Francisco, Pack Some Giant Lasers

Ginormica survives robot's crushing claws

A giant alien robot is poised to attack San Francisco. The president and army were unable to contain the threat at the landing site. Astronomers speculate that the strange blip they reported recently must have been the alien robot coming to Earth.

Neither General Monger nor the office of President Hathaway could be reached for comment. The nation is shocked.

"I trusted the president to protect us. Now what will we do?" asked one concerned citizen.

Aliens really do exist!

EPIC BAT
GOLDEN

TLE AT
GATE BRIDGE

It's been a week of shocking revelations. Aliens exist, the government can't stop them, and, lucky for us, the rumored monsters are real—and on our side!

As the alien robot smashed into San Francisco, Californians were treated to an unusual sight. A nearly fifty-foot woman came to the rescue. Ginormica, as she is known, was not only able to defeat the alien robot, she was also able to save many innocent bystanders stranded on the Golden Gate Bridge.

Ginormica, however, would not take all the credit. "I couldn't have done it without the help of my friends The Missing Link, B.O.B., Dr. Cockroach, PhD, and Insectosaurus," she said. "They are the true heroes. If they hadn't taught me to believe in myself, I could never have done what I did."

EXCLUSIVE INTERVIEW with
THE MISSING LINK!

THE MISSING LINK: still ready to fight the bad guys

We were lucky enough to ask The Missing Link a few questions before he disappeared into the deep end of the pool.

The ReExaminer: Mr. Link, would you care to tell us a little bit about yourself?

The Missing Link: Well, I want to assure you all that although I may not swim as fast or climb as high as I used to a million years ago, I'm still ready to fight the bad guys.

RE: Great! Now, your appearance— it's so . . . interesting.

TML: Thanks, I like to think I look pretty good. Did you know that pond scum is good for your skin?

As a reward for saving the Earth from a giant alien robot, the monsters have been granted their freedom by the president himself and were released to enjoy normal life.

The team's first public appearance was with the family of Susan Murphy, aka Ginormica, at their home. Friends and neighbors were invited to celebrate with a barbeque in the backyard.

MONSTERS ARE TRUE HEROES!

The monsters have been granted their freedom.

The monsters reportedly had some trouble making new friends. One departing guest was quoted as saying, "AAAAAAAH!"

However, some felt it was a success. "I think the pudding likes me," said B.O.B.

BIG HEARTBREAK

Ginormica used her first moments of freedom to reunite with her true love, weatherman Derek Dietl. However, a tearful Ginormica later reported that the relationship was kaput and that Derek had documentation to show that the marriage wasn't official.

Will Aliens Attack Again?

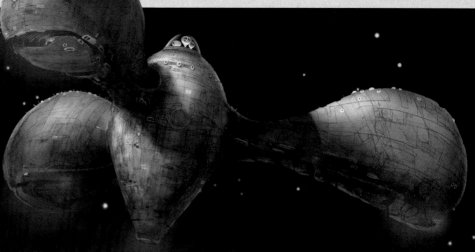

Spaceship Spotted by Gas-station Attendant

Jimmy Jones doesn't get out much. He spends his days pumping gas and selling candy bars. But yesterday he spotted something unusual . . . and it may mean aliens will attack again! "I saw a bright light," said Jones. "And then this giant woman was beamed up into a spaceship! And then this huge bug creature shot snot out of its nose!"

When asked if the giant woman and bug creature matched descriptions of the monsters who recently saved the city of San Francisco, Jones replied, "I don't know. I've never been to San Francisco."

ARTIST'S RENDERING

FBI Releases Alien Profile

Name: *Gallaxhar*

Description: *Part humanoid, part squid, all alien*

Goal: *To locate quantonium, a substance that will give him great power*

Plans: *To use the quantonium to replicate himself and take over the universe with his "army of me"*

Once again the motley crew of heroic monsters is preparing for battle, this time with a more formidable enemy. The government has confirmed that San Francisco heroes Ginormica, The Missing Link, Dr. Cockroach, PhD, B.O.B., and Insectosaurus have been deployed to battle alien Gallaxhar and put an end to his evil plans.

Meanwhile, scientists revealed that they have studied the meteor that changed Susan Murphy into Ginormica and found an unknown substance inside the alien rock. "We've identified this rare substance as quantonium," one scientist said.

There are unconfirmed rumors circulating that Gallaxhar is planning to use the quantonium to create his own alien army.

MONSTERS TO THE RESCUE?

VICTORY

Monsters Defeat Interstellar Threat

The monster team traveled to outer space to confront the alien, Gallaxhar, on his own turf. They destroyed his spaceship and everything on it.

The monsters used their smarts and their acting skills as they impersonated Gallaxhar clones to infiltrate the high-security regions of his spaceship.

The Missing Link and B.O.B. heroically fought off the clones, while Dr. Cockroach

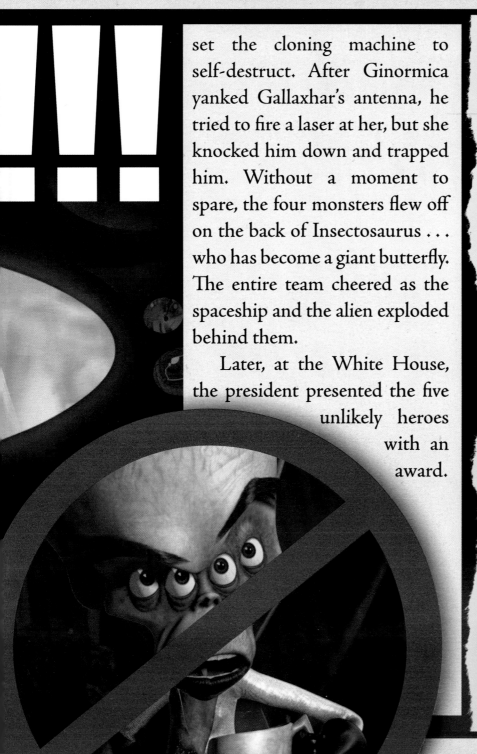

!!!

set the cloning machine to self-destruct. After Ginormica yanked Gallaxhar's antenna, he tried to fire a laser at her, but she knocked him down and trapped him. Without a moment to spare, the four monsters flew off on the back of Insectosaurus . . . who has become a giant butterfly. The entire team cheered as the spaceship and the alien exploded behind them.

Later, at the White House, the president presented the five unlikely heroes with an award.

President Hathaway's Speech

"Job well done, monsters. The Earth has been saved and we owe it all to you. In appreciation of your efforts, we would like to return you to a maximum-security prison of your choice. . . . what's that? Oh, old speech. Sorry!

On behalf of the world, monsters, I would like to present you with the Presidential Beads of Gratitude."

OFF INTO THE SUNSET

After another job well done, the monster crew is being treated to some well-earned rest. A government spokeswoman said they have been taken to an undisclosed location—a top secret resort where they can get some rest and relaxation.

"I'm just delighted to have my own giant little cottage away from it all," Ginormica gushed over the phone.

Citizens of the world are happy to reward the monsters with some peace and quiet. That is, until they are needed again.